Billy Blackfeet in the Rockies

A Story from History

by **Marc Simmons**
illustrations by **Ronald Kil**

University of New Mexico Press • Albuquerque

Text © 2006 by Marc Simmons
Illustrations © 2006 by Ronald Kil
All rights reserved. Published 2006
Printed in Hong Kong by Toppan Printing Company, Inc.
12 11 10 09 08 07 06   1 2 3 4 5 6 7

LIBRARY OF CONGRESS CATALOGING-IN-PUBLICATION DATA

Simmons, Marc.
Billy Blackfeet in the Rockies : a story from history /
Marc Simmons ; illustrated by Ronald Kil.
p. cm. — (Children of the West series)
Summary: A fur-trading post for the Blackfeet Indians is home to
Billy Jackson and his family in the Montana of 1864,
as the ten-year-old faces danger from man, beast, and nature.
ISBN-13: 978-0-8263-4105-1 (CLOTH : ALK. PAPER)
ISBN-10: 0-8263-4105-5 (CLOTH : ALK. PAPER)
1. Frontier and pioneer life—Fiction. 2. Sihasapa Indians—Fiction.
3. Indians of North America—Great Plains—Fiction.
1. Montana—History—19th century—Fiction. I. Kil, Ronald R., 1959– ill.
II. Title. III. Series: Simmons, Marc. Children of the West series.
PZ7.S591855Bil 2006
[FIC]—dc22

2006003860

Series design by Robyn Mundy
Book design and layout by Kathleen Sparkes
Body type is Trump Mediaeval 12/22
Display type is Bodoni Poster and Officina Serif

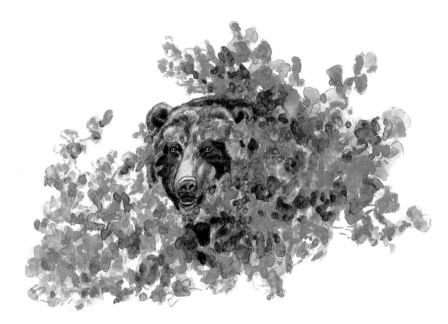

To Clayton Harrison Smaltz,
I hope you grow up to be like Billy.
—Ron Kil

Foreword

Fort Benton, Montana, on the Missouri River, 1864.
A fur-trading post for the Blackfeet Indians.

Once each year in early spring a steamboat came up the river from St. Louis. It brought a new supply of trade goods for the fort. A big celebration always greeted the arrival of the boat.

William (Billy) Jackson was born at Fort Benton. He spent his first ten years at this busy outpost on the wild frontier. It was the only home he knew. Here, everyone used the Blackfeet language. Billy spoke Blackfeet before he learned English.

Billy's beloved grandfather Hugh Monroe worked as a hunter for Fort Benton. He supplied the deer, antelope, and buffalo meat that fed its forty employees.

In his early years Hugh Monroe had come west and joined the Blackfeet tribe. Soon he talked and dressed like the Indians. He also married a chief's daughter, Fox Woman, who became Billy's grandmother. She always called her husband by his Indian name, Rising Wolf.

This is the story of what happened to Billy, his grandfather Rising Wolf, and their family in 1864. Billy always remembered it as a year of tragedy. At the same time, he learned the meaning of bravery. That was something he never forgot.

People in This Story

Billy Jackson—A boy who has much to learn about the mountain wilderness.

Robert Jackson—Billy's brother, two years older.

Thomas Jackson—Father of Billy and Robert; a clerk at Fort Benton.

Amelia Jackson—Mother of Billy; the half-Blackfeet wife of Thomas Jackson.

Rising Wolf (Hugh Monroe)—Grandfather of Billy; father of Amelia, Lizzie, and Frank.

Fox Woman—Grandmother of Billy; the wise and beautiful wife of Rising Wolf.

Indians

Blackfeet—A large and powerful tribe of Montana and southern Canada that adopted Hugh Monroe.

Assiniboins—A fierce people of the Canadian border who often raided the Blackfeet.

Kutenais—A mountain tribe, small in numbers. Friends of the Blackfeet.

"Billy! Get up. You can't sleep all day," the boy's mother Amelia called to him in the Blackfeet language.

Yawning, Billy tumbled out of his bunk. "I'm coming, Mother," he replied in Blackfeet.

The whole Jackson family had been up late the night before. The yearly steamboat from St. Louis had reached Fort Benton at noon. That set off a noisy welcome. When Billy finally went to bed, the fort workers were still singing loudly and playing their fiddles.

After his mother's call, Billy put on his clothes. Then he went straight to the breakfast table.

"Good morning, son," Mr. Jackson said with a soft voice. "I'm glad it didn't take fireworks to get you out of bed."

Billy's brother Robert, sleepy-eyed, walked into the kitchen. "Sit down, boys," their father told them. I have some bad news that came with the steamboat."

"And you'd better hear this too, Amelia," Thomas Jackson said to his wife.

"Now here is what your grandfather, Rising Wolf, and I have been told. The government has not renewed the business license of the Fur Company. This means that without a license Fort Benton can no longer trade with the Indians."

Billy was startled. He didn't fully understand what he was hearing. But by the grim look on his father's face, he knew it was something very serious.

"The fort will be closed down after this last steamboat load of goods is sold," Mr. Jackson explained to his family. "So your grandfather and I will be out of our jobs. We will all have to leave and go somewhere else to find work."

There was no mistaking the meaning of that. A cold fear swept over Billy. The Jacksons were about to lose their home!

Mr. Jackson got up from the table. He put on his blue company jacket with the brass buttons. Then he left for his day in the Fort Benton trading store.

His words had greatly alarmed the boys. So they followed him to work, hoping that their father would tell them not to worry . . . and that he would find a new home for them.

The store was crowded with Blackfeet Indians ready to trade. They had arrived the day before and pitched their tepees just outside the fort. Now the Indians held up soft buffalo robes, and skins of deer, elk, and beaver. These furs were their money to buy the whiteman's goods.

Inside the log store, a counter ran the length of the room. Behind it, wooden shelves were filled with groceries, hardware, rolls of cloth, packets of needles, strings of beads, and many other things.

Mr. Jackson was suddenly very busy and had no time for his sons.

"We must go see Grandfather," whispered Billy. "He'll know what's to become of us."

Robert thought for a moment. He loved the noisy trading that went on in the store. When he got older, he wanted to be a clerk, just like his father. So it was hard to leave now with all the business going on at the counter.

For once, though, Robert agreed with his younger brother. "Well, come on then," he said, as if it were his idea. "We'll talk to Rising Wolf."

The two of them soon found their grandfather. He was in the fort's blacksmith shop watching the smith nail an iron shoe on a horse's hoof.

When Rising Wolf saw Billy and Robert, he came over and spoke to them.

"Aha, now! I see from your worried faces that you know Fort Benton will be closing down."

Both his grandsons nodded their heads.

"Well, come with me outside the fort," said Rising Wolf. "I want to show you where we are going."

The three of them passed through Fort Benton's big gate. Then they walked to the edge of the grassy plain. The land rolled westward to distant mountains.

"There," exclaimed Rising Wolf, pointing with his finger. "To those steep mountains I will take my children and grandsons. It's time you boys learned to hunt and trap. For too long you have lived inside fort walls."

"Your next lessons will be given in the wild country of the Rocky Mountains. We'll take two tepees," Rising Wolf added. "It's time we lived like Blackfeet for a while."

"Hurrah for the shining mountains!" Billy shouted with excitement.

As far back as he could remember, Billy Jackson had gazed at those faraway peaks from the walls of Fort Benton. Now he and Robert were going there, guided by Grandfather Rising Wolf.

It took a week to prepare for the trip. Fox Woman and her daughters Amelia and Lizzie packed the family's clothes in painted rawhide boxes. They gathered up cooking pots and water buckets. And they folded the skin tepee covers to prepare them for travel.

Rising Wolf, with his son Frank, sharpened the knives and axes, mended old traps and bought new ones. Billy and Robert tagged along when Grandfather traded for extra horses in the Blackfeet camp.

At dawn on the day to go, Billy jumped from his bunk. The first thing he saw was a small, brand-new rifle. It lay atop his folded clothes.

"Robert! Robert! Wake up," Billy called joyously. "Look, you have a rifle, too. Father has given them to us, so we can become hunters."

Later that morning, Rising Wolf gave the proud boys a warning. "Now a rifle is a dangerous tool. You will learn to handle it carefully. So for now, neither of you will load and fire your gun unless I am with you."

The boys would soon forget his words.

Almost everyone in the fort came out to see Rising Wolf and his family leave for the mountains.

"Look at Father," Robert exclaimed. For once Mr. Jackson was not wearing his blue jacket with the brass buttons. Instead, he was dressed like a trapper in a blanket-coat and a hood.

Billy thought his father looked awkward climbing into the saddle. Mr. Jackson was not an outdoorsman. He had never set a beaver trap or hunted with a rifle. He didn't seem to fit in.

Two dozen horses were loaded with camp equipment. They formed the main part of the family's caravan. Some of the horses pulled a travois. A travois was made of two poles that dragged on the ground. Indians used it to move heavy things, like the leather coverings for tepees and rawhide boxes of clothing and dried buffalo meat.

Rising Wolf's twenty-year-old daughter Lizzie had eagerly helped in loading the horses. She was always the first to volunteer for difficult jobs. Billy loved his Aunt Lizzie for her strength, courage, and happy nature. Uncle Frank, Lizzie's brother, was not like that. He worked hard but was quiet and seldom spoke to the boys.

Under bright morning sunlight, the caravan moved out. Grandfather Rising Wolf rode in the lead with Fox Woman and Amelia. Thomas Jackson and his sons herded the travois and pack animals. Lizzie and Frank brought up the rear, driving a band of spare horses.

The family dogs helped move the caravan along with their barking.

For two days the family pushed across the open plains. Buffalo and antelope ran to get out of the way. Seeing them, Billy decided, "Yes! I want to be a hunter just like Grandfather."

At the end of the second day, they reached the edge of tall mountains. The mouth of a long, green valley opened before them. Inside the valley was the bluest lake that Billy and Robert had ever seen.

"Here we will set up our hunting camp," announced Rising Wolf. "The women will pitch two tepees on the shore. Tomorrow we will build a log corral. The corral will hold our horses at night, so that an enemy war party will have trouble stealing them."

After the evening meal in the Jackson tepee, Billy said to his mother Amelia, "I'm glad now we left the fort and came here."

"It is a good place for you and Robert to learn how we Blackfeet live in the mountains," she replied. "This beautiful water where we are camped is called the Two Medicine Lake in our language."

Billy smiled when he heard that. He wanted to know the Blackfeet name for every mountain and stream. Amelia would teach her son their names on this hunting trip.

The following day the men and boys worked hard on the horse corral. They cut posts and set them in the ground. Then they tied straight pine rails to the posts with rawhide straps. By noon the corral was finished.

In the afternoon Rising Wolf said, "I have something to do up the valley. I'll return before dark."

"Oh, can we go with you, Grandfather?" begged Billy and Robert.

"All right," answered Rising Wolf. "Bring your new rifles. But you are not to use them without my permission. And stay close to me at all times. There are many dangers in these mountains."

The three left camp on foot. Walking fast, they followed an old Indian trail that led deeper into the high country. Patches of late winter snow still lay in the shadows of soaring cliffs.

When Rising Wolf and the two boys came to a little stream, they stopped. Along the banks were pine trees and cottonwoods.

Billy watched as his grandfather cut some bark away with his hunting knife. It left a bare white circle on a tree trunk.

"Now watch closely, boys," the old man told them. Then he took out of a sack some lumps of black charcoal from last night's campfire.

"You are going to make marks on the tree," Billy guessed.

"Not just marks, Grandson. I'm going to make my picture sign." And Rising Wolf began to draw with the charcoal. Soon he had formed the upper part of a man. Below it he drew a wolf.

"In case any Blackfeet pass by, they will see the sign of Rising Wolf. They will not raid our camp by mistake, thinking we are enemies."

Still farther up the valley,
Grandfather stopped again to make
another sign.

But by now the boys had lost
interest. Bored, they slipped away
unnoticed and wandered up the
Indian trail, pretending to be hunters.

Animal tracks could be seen everywhere
on the ground. "Here are deer tracks," Billy called out.

Robert, excited now, said, "I'm oldest. I get the first shot when
we find one."

About then, the two came upon a thick clump of tall bushes. They
heard a grunting noise and saw some dark brown fur behind the branches.

"It must be a buffalo," cried Billy. In the next moment, his brother
fired his brand-new rifle.

The shot made a long echo down the green valley. A terrific roar came from the bushes.

Robert's bullet had hit something. But not a buffalo. Suddenly a giant grizzly bear burst into sight. Both boys were terrified.

The bear stood up on its hind legs, eyes red in anger. It opened its mighty jaws to roar again. The boys saw the rows of white teeth and huge claws on the front paws.

Robert turned and ran like the north wind. That left little Billy alone, facing the bear.

Bravely, Billy Jackson raised his rifle. Slowly, he took aim as his hands shook. He fired, striking the bear in its side.

Still the animal did not fall. Instead, it gave another terrible howl and rushed at the boy.

Now it was Billy's turn to run. Off he raced as fast as his short legs could carry him. The wounded grizzly followed close at his heels.

"Help! Help me, Rising Wolf," yelled Billy. He knew he was about to be caught and eaten by the bear. The boy very much wished he had obeyed his grandfather and not wandered off to hunt.

Then Billy saw a large cottonwood tree. One of its branches dipped low toward the ground. He made a flying leap and grabbed the branch with both hands. His legs dangled in the air.

The snarling bear reached up with a mighty paw. One of its razor-sharp claws slashed Billy's trouser leg and cut the flesh.

"In another minute," Billy thought, "this big bear is gonna eat me for his dinner."

All at once a rifle boomed. The grizzly bear dropped to the ground, lifeless, as Rising Wolf dashed up. Billy, weak and hurting, let go of the tree branch. He fell to the ground.

Robert now came running. "Just look at that grizzly we got. He must be the biggest bear in the Rocky Mountains," the youngster boasted loudly.

"Robert Jackson! William Jackson! I can't believe you two boys are my grandsons," thundered Rising Wolf. His eyes flashed with anger.

"You didn't listen to what I told you to do. And Robert, you almost got your brother killed. Sneak off from me again and I'll take away your rifles for the rest of the summer," Grandfather warned them sternly.

Robert was so excited over getting the bear that he paid no attention to the scolding. The scolding hurt Billy deeply, however. More than anything else, he wanted to please Rising Wolf. But instead, because of his thoughtless behavior, he had made his grandfather furious.

"You boys help me skin out this bear," Rising
Wolf ordered gruffly.

He and Robert went to work with their hunting
knives. Billy got up from the ground where he had fallen.
His bloody leg hurt and he felt sick from his recent scare.
Yet, without complaining, he joined in the skinning.

Their return to camp with the bearskin caused a stir.
Mr. Jackson was upset when he heard that his sons had
shot a grizzly. Fox Woman and the boys' mother Amelia
both said that Blackfeet believe a bearskin brings bad luck.
They refused to tan it.

Just then Lizzie came up from the lake with a bucket
of water. "I'm not afraid of bad luck," she declared. "I'll tan
that bear hide to make a bed cover for my nephews."

Rising Wolf smiled and said, "Good for you, Lizzie.
At least somebody in this camp is brave."

In the early days of April that followed, Rising Wolf and his family worked hard at trapping beaver. Once Billy was out alone with his grandfather just after sunrise.

They were walking along the edge of the lake when they heard loud splashing sounds. A bull moose suddenly appeared. It was wading in the shallow water near shore.

Billy gasped. Never had he seen such a proud animal. Its furry coat gleamed in the early sunlight.

As the boy stared at the moose, his chest swelled with happiness. "I love this wilderness," he said to himself.

Woman's Saddle

Pipe and Pipe Bag

There were other days when Billy got to spend time alone with Fox Woman. As she worked, his grandmother told him about the Blackfeet people: what they believed and how they lived before the whitemen came.

Billy heard all about Napi, or "Old Man," who had created the world from a ball of mud. Then with the help of "Old Woman," his wife, Napi created people and all other living things.

"Grandson," Fox Woman said to him, "here is a Blackfeet song you need to know." Then she sang a hunting song that men sang before going out to find wild game.

"Learn the Blackfeet way of doing things," she told him. "Your brother Robert cares nothing for this. But you are different. Billy, in your heart you are a true Blackfeet."

Fire Starting Kit

flint

steel

tinder

Spring moved forward. The last snow banks along the Indian trail melted.

Week by week, the family's packs of beaver fur grew.

"At this rate, we'll soon be rich," Rising Wolf predicted.

He spoke to Billy's father about his plans. "We should return to Fort Benton while it is still doing business. We can sell the furs, buy supplies, then decide how we'll spend the coming summer." Mr. Jackson agreed and nodded his head.

As Rising Wolf explained it, the plan sounded simple. But two nights later disaster struck. And after that, nothing was ever the same again.

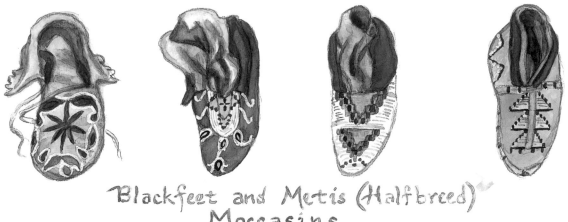

Blackfeet and Metis (Halfbreed) Moccasins

The family was feasting in the evening on roast buffalo, called *nitápi waksen* in Blackfeet, meaning "real food." They had gathered inside Rising Wolf and Fox Woman's large tepee. Billy sat between Lizzie and Rising Wolf by the fire. He couldn't remember when he'd felt so happy.

All at once their dogs started barking loudly at the horse corral.

"Maybe they have found a bear," Lizzie said.

"Or more likely some horse thieves," her brother Frank answered.

Frank picked up his rifle and hurried into the darkness. Mr. Jackson, Robert, and Billy raced to their tepee to get their own guns.

As they did, they heard a bang! bang! from the direction of the corral. Then came shouts in a strange language that Billy did not understand.

His father recognized it, though. "Assiniboins," he exclaimed. "The worst enemies of the Blackfeet and they are taking our horses."

Returning, the three of them found Rising Wolf in front of his tepee. He was telling the women to run for the woods and hide there in the bushes.

Fox Woman refused. "Those Assiniboins are going to kill you. I want to fight and die at your side," she said in a shaking voice.

"I have no time to argue, Fox Woman. You all must go, and fast," her husband ordered. Without another word, the women headed for the trees.

As Rising Wolf led Mr. Jackson and the boys toward the corral, more gunshots broke out. They found Frank firing toward the log gate.

In that instant, one of the raiders cut the rawhide rope holding the gate. It opened and the frightened horses came spilling out.

"The herd is scattering," Rising Wolf whispered. "Our enemies will try to round up as many as they can in the dark. Let's spread out and see if we can't recover a few of the horses ourselves."

Billy tried to follow his grandfather. Quickly he ran out of breath and found himself alone. Filled with fear, he felt his knees shaking.

Then Billy heard a noise behind him. It was his Aunt Lizzie and she was carrying a rifle.

"I know I'm disobeying Rising Wolf," she told him. "But I can fight and so I will." Her bold words thrilled Billy. They helped him defeat his fear and regain his courage.

Together, aunt and nephew went in search of horses.

By now a full moon had risen in the east. Like a giant lamp it lit up the valley.

Through a clump of pines came two Assiniboins, riding stolen horses. Lizzie signaled Billy, and they both raised their rifles, firing at once. The Assiniboins fell to the ground.

The horses, now riderless, ran loose. Somehow Billy and his aunt each caught one and scrambled aboard.

"Follow me," shouted Lizzie. They dashed on horseback across the valley floor. Six more Assiniboins chased them, shooting bullets and arrows.

Lizzie led the way toward a rushing river in the upper end of the valley. At its edge, they stopped and looked down into foaming rapids. Above the roar of the water, they could hear the war cries of their enemies.

Billy was scared half to death, as he had been when he faced the grizzly bear. But as Aunt Lizzie guided her horse into the dark water, she yelled to him: "*Ikakimat! Ikakimat!*" ("Take courage! Take courage, nephew!")

Bravely, he followed Lizzie and her horse into the swirling river. White waves washed over them as the pair held on to their horses' manes. The strong animals, swimming, finally got them to the other side. Billy and Lizzie were safe.

The Assiniboins had stopped to watch, expecting the woman and boy to drown. When that didn't happen, the Assiniboins gave up the chase.

Lizzie and Billy climbed a ridge with the horses, wishing to circle around to their camp. On top, Lizzie cried out: "Look at those two orange lights below us. The Assiniboins are burning our tepees."

And it was true. When they got back, Billy saw that the raiders were gone. His family with sad faces was standing by the smoking remains of the tepees. Everything had been stolen or burned, including the furs they had worked so hard to trap.

"Oooooh," Lizzie wailed in distress. Billy, shocked by the terrible sight, made no sound. A sharp pain grew in his chest. It was the beginning of his grief for what they had lost.

"We are ruined," groaned Mr. Jackson. "There's nothing left but the clothes we are wearing, our rifles, and the two horses Billy and Lizzie brought in. That's all!"

"The only thing I care about," Rising Wolf said with relief, "is that I still have all my family. Given the fight we had, that is a miracle."

Soon after dawn, Rising Wolf and his family started slowly down the valley. Before long they came across a tepee camp of Kutenais Indians. These people had crossed over from the west slope of the Rockies to find better hunting.

The band leader welcomed Rising Wolf, saying: "We are sorry to hear of the troubles our Blackfeet friends have had with those Assiniboin raiders. We shall feed you well. Then we will send you on your journey with many gifts."

True to his words, the Kutenais gave the party of Blackfeet strangers some horses, saddles, camp equipment, and even a tepee.

Two days more of travel and Billy Jackson saw the walls of Fort Benton rise into view.

It was not long before the few people left in the fort knew of Rising Wolf's misfortune. Several offered to lend him money for a new trapping expedition.

Shortly, he announced that he would take his family into Canada. There they would hunt and trap with the northern Blackfeet.

"No! Oh, no! Not again," Thomas Jackson declared firmly. "That life is too dangerous. I've had enough of it." In fact, he had heard of a clerking job at a trading post down the Missouri River.

"Billy. Robert. We are leaving by boat tomorrow. I'm going back to the work I know best," their father told them.

The boys were stunned. Of course, they had to go with their father and mother into a new life, and part with their grandparents

Early the next morning Rising Wolf, Fox Woman, Frank, and Lizzie gathered at the boat landing to say good-bye. Many years would pass before Billy and Robert would see them again.

Billy stood for a time next to his grandfather, with the old man's hand on his shoulder. The boy hoped no one noticed the tears forming in his eyes.

His brother Robert was happily chattering about the coming boat trip. But Billy thought only of this breaking apart of his family.

His father called him to get in the small boat. And Rising Wolf said to his grandson: "Come back to us one day, Billy. Just like me, you belong with the Blackfeet."

Hearing those words, Billy Jackson tried to smile as he climbed into the boat. But the smile would not come. Then Rising Wolf, Fox Woman, Frank, and Lizzie were gone.

Billy was left only with the warm memory of their hunting trip together in the mountains, when he had faced a grizzly bear and a dangerous river crossing with Lizzie. Those things Billy Jackson would remember always.

William Jackson
(Billy Blackfeet)
and
General Custer 1876

Afterword

William (Billy) and Robert Jackson lived for a number of years at Fort Buford in western North Dakota, where their father was chief clerk in the trading post.

In their late teens, the boys enlisted as army scouts and afterward saw duty in wars with the Sioux (Lakota), Cheyenne, and other Plains tribes.

Both accompanied General George A. Custer's large expedition to the Little Big Horn River in 1876. They escaped death at the historic battle there only because they were serving with Major Marcus Reno's separate division of the expedition.

William Jackson with his wife and children in later years had a fine ranch on the Cut Bank River in Montana. He died at age forty-nine in 1903, a victim of tuberculosis.

Sources

This book, like the other titles in the Children of the West Series, is based upon actual events in the life of a real child. The aim of the series is to inspire young readers by offering them examples of courage in the face of danger and adversity. Certain small details have been altered and dialogue created in developing this story.

We would know little in the life of William (Billy) Jackson were it not for the writings of James Willard Schultz. In 1877 Schultz came up the Missouri River to Fort Benton, Montana, where he fell under the spell of the Blackfeet Indians. He knew both William Jackson and Hugh Monroe (Rising Wolf) and from them heard their life stories. See his books *William Jackson, Indian Scout* (1926), and *Rising Wolf, The White Blackfoot* (1918).

Both men also receive attention in Schultz's *My Life as an Indian* (1935), and *Many Strange Characters* (1982). For the history and culture of the Blackfeet tribe consult John C. Ewers, *The Blackfeet, Raiders of the Northwestern Plains* (1958).

Some years ago, the Blackfeet Tribal Council resolved that they should no longer be referred to as "Blackfoot," as was often done, but the plural "Blackfeet" would be the official name of the tribe.